ANTS IN YER PANTS

Written by Chris Mac
Illustrated by Gary B

HENDERSON
PUBLISHING LTD
© 1997 HENDERSON PUBLISHING LTD

Bored again? Nothing to do and nowhere to go? Mad Jack's got a brilliant new idea. **ANTS IN YER PANTS**. Sounds crazy? Let's find out.

Most people don't know a lot about creepies. Four legs and furry is about as much as they can handle. Whenever something really interesting scoots over the floor or up the wall everyone but you gets busy looking somewhere else. And if you do happen to mention it they get that funny look in their eyes. Sometimes they run out of the room screaming.

A lot of people - especially adults - seriously think everything with more than four legs or less than two is called a yuck. They're always saying it.

Look at that...yuck.

They don't know what they're missing.

Bug is another yuck-type name, which is a pity because it's such a great word. The problem is there really **ARE** things called bugs. This is very confusing. When is a bug not a bug? The answer is...when it's a beetle - or a spider - or a fly - or an ant - or a centipede - or a woodlouse - or a something-else. Unless it does happen to be a bug, of course.

So what IS a bug **?**

You'll see.

And you'll see a whole lot more. Once you start looking - **REALLY** looking - you'll see some of the weirdest, craziest, **WILDEST** animals in the world. Nothing will ever be the same again.

GEARING UP

Mad Jack's pooter-pot is nearly all you need to get started. It's a breeze. Suck it and see.

But what <u>is</u> a pooter ?
A pooter is Mad Jack's essential entomological aid as it helps him to inspect the insects he has caught without hurting them, and without them hurting him!

What you need:
a pot with a lid, two different coloured bendy drinking straws, some sticking plaster, a scrap of muslin or net curtain, and small rubber bands or thread.

First of all you'll need to make two holes in the lid to push the straws through. They should fit tightly, but you can use sticking plaster to fix them if the holes are too big. Push one straw in deep. Now fix the muslin or net over the end of the other straw before you push it in. Then put the top on the pot and **ABRACADABRA** there is your pooter. Prepare to be daring!

Practise on lentils or a few grains of rice. Put the short tube near your target and suck suddenly through the long tube.

4

ONE CRUCIAL RULE
NEVER SUCK THROUGH THE SHORT TUBE. If you do, you could get a mouthful of furious thingies.

Yummy!

A short, sharp 'tf' works better than a long, slow huff. Leggy thingies have to be plucked off their feet before they get time to think: 'Oh-oh, it's getting a bit windy. Better hang on tight.'

NO!

They have to scoot through the tube straight into the pot before they get time to think: 'Um. Interesting tunnel. Let's stop and have a wander round.'

If this does happen, wait for the thingy to decide which way it wants to go. If it crawls out you can easily poot it up again; if it crawls in, it's in. Blowing into your pooter will make it all wet and steamy inside. This makes it very hard to see what you've got. Whatever's in there will also get stuck down and desperate!

And what else do you need...?

1 **Eyes.** Don't leave home without them.

2 **Old, comfortable clothes with plenty of old, comfortable pockets.**

plus

1 **Pencil.** Mainly for poking things you don't want to touch (add a notebook if you like making notes).

2 **Spare pot(s).** Plastic beats glass (which is heavy and can break), push-on tops beat screw tops (which need two hands - think about it).

3 **Plastic bags.** (Not the sort with little round holes in, purlease!)

5

WHERE TO LOOK

One great thing about thingy-hunting is that it doesn't matter where you live. Thingies lurk everywhere - indoors and out.

The wild wood is an obvious place to go. So is the park, and the garden, and the backyard...

...but what if you live in a town with no woods, no park, no garden, not even a back yard?

Well, there has to be a windowsill, maybe even a balcony. If there's an attic, cellar, boiler-room or laundry-room, there you go. Even without one of these glory-holes you could still find thingies to poot indoors. Most homes have loads more creepies in them than people (sssh! don't tell the people).

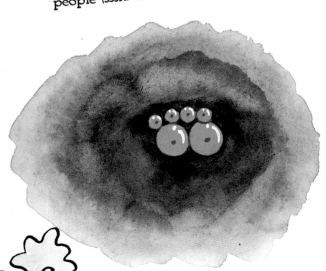

Creepies hide in corners and cracks. Houses are full of corners, and there are cracks everywhere - between floorboards, under the fridge, out on the street... There could even be a sturdy tree out there, or something else working at being green and growing.

Creepies crawl under things. Outdoors, turn over stones and chunks of wood (but don't forget to put them back afterwards). Poke under flaky tree-bark. Indoors, peer under the doormat and poot behind loose wallpaper. Use your imagination: imagine you're a natural-born creepy and think where you'd go to get away from voracious vacuum cleaners and dire dusters.

Least favourite places are very dry, very cold, very clean, and very busy. Favourite places are dark, damp and undisturbed. It's not hard to make somewhere like this - try leaving an old book out on the windowsill for a week or two...(make sure the family knows what you're doing so it doesn't get tidied away).

Fantastic foreign creepies sometimes arrive in boxes of fruit and veg from around the world. Mad Jack asked the fruit shop people to tell him if any turned up there. Naturally, they like stamping on thingies first and scraping the mess off the floor second, so it wasn't easy to get them interested (grovel grovel, cringe cringe) but it was worth it. The very first thing he got was a spider from Africa!

Once you've got some, the ultimate designer-home for creepies is a terrarium. You can put anything you find in here - and keep it in your own room where it won't scare everyone.

MAKING A

An old aquarium is perfect. Ask around. Somebody might have a plastic one that got cracked - even if it doesn't hold water it'll be okay for damp soil.

If you can't get an aquarium, use any big strong box (or even a giant jar) with see-through sides. All that really matters is to have enough air, the right amount of moisture, and no holes big enough for your smallest guests to squirm through.

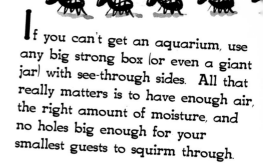

The lid is important because it has to let air in without letting creepies out. It should also be easy to get on and off because you may need to put food and new guests in and clear out old mouldy stuff nearly every day. With a big terrarium, it's a good idea to make a serving hatch.

If you're using a jar, throw away the lid it came with and stretch a piece of fine netting (old net curtain is perfect) across the top with a rubber band.

8

TeRRaRIuM

Unless your main aim is an ants' nest (see p. 12), keep the terrarium away from direct heat (e.g. radiators, sun, and the back of the **TV**). It's always best to have it away from direct light (e.g. sun and the front of the **TV**). Put it where you want it to go **BEFORE** you put anything in, because it's going to be **HEAVY** (so choose a **STRONG** place with **STRONG** legs).

NO SUN...
... NO T.V.
(SNIFF)

S p r e a d

some clean gravel and stones on the bottom, then half-fill with crumbly-moist soil (dry soil for ants). Add a few interesting things - a brick or stone, some twigs and dead wood, maybe even a clump of grass. If anyone starts getting suspicious you can say it's art.

ANTS

Ants can be black, yellow, brown or red. They live nearly everywhere and nearly everyhow, but nobody knows everything about them. Anyone could discover something new, anytime - it could be you!

Where to go anting...
In the country: no problemo. In town: parks, back yards, playgrounds (especially grungy sandpits), between paving-stones. Watch out for clues such as loose soil and little holes.

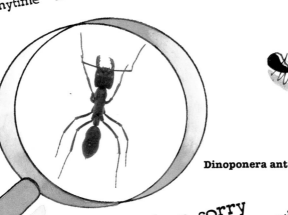

Dinoponera ant

Better safe than sorry

Soldier ants bite. Red ants also squirt acid that can blister your skin. Ant acid can burn your lungs if you breathe it in, so pooting red ants isn't such a great idea. The big red ones that make mounds in the forest have acid plus a ferocious bite. This is a pain, but not seriously dangerous. But a few ants ARE dangerous: beware American bearded ants (they sting like wasps), and don't go NEAR giant Australian bulldog ants - they bite AND sting AND jump!

10

Most of the ants you'll see running around are the little ones that do the work. They're called workers (surprise surprise!) and they're all females.

Those jaws are weapons. They're about as much use for eating dinner as a sub-machine-gun; some extra-tough soldiers have to be fed like babies by the workers.

If the nest is attacked (like when you kick it or poke it - or sit on it by mistake) soldiers rush out to defend their city. They're females too (yes they are). While you're beating them off, try to remember why you came and poot up a few for a closer look.

If your kick damaged the nursery, you'll also see workers running around rescuing eggs and babies.

Now watch and wait. See how the ants clear up the mess and repair the damage, and how long it takes.

11

ant's nest

Kicking an ants' nest is like bombing a city. All you get to see is how they handle a mega-emergency - and if you think that's impressive, just wait until you get a chance to spy on what else they can do! Getting the inside story on ant city isn't the easiest thing in the world, but it's well worth the effort.

Somewhere

in the heart of the nest there'll be one or more queens. A queen lives in her own chamber, busily laying eggs. Every ant in the nest is a queen's child, but very few are princesses. They're nearly all females, but queens are the only females who ever get to mate - and they only do it once.

Most of the eggs hatch into workers, which is how ant city grows. A few become new queens, and just a few more will be drones. These are the males, who have just one job to do and only get one day's work in their whole life! After that, they die.

*O*ne day in the summer the new queens come out and fly away. All the males go after them, flying up and up, trying to catch a queen and mate with her. This is when the thingies called 'flying ants' suddenly come from nowhere and people run around shouting 'yuck!'

*W*hen it happens, don't dive for cover like everybody else. Go for a jam jar instead, because this is your big chance. This is the time you can catch a queen and get your very own ants' nest to watch.

The clever name for an ant terrarium is a formicarium.

BOSS

*Q*ueens are bigger than drones - about the size of a small bee. After mating, they come down and look for a place to start a nest, rubbing off their wings as they go. Look on the ground for a fertilized queen. You may find her with or without wings on, or with just one or two left out of the four she started with.

13

SETTING THE QUEEN UP

When you've got a queen, you can simply tip her into a warm, dark terrarium and let her get on with it. But if you want to watch what she does, you need to make a thin vertical sandwich of loose dry soil between two sheets of rigid plastic.

the **Queen** raises her first little gang of workers all alone. She lives off the meat in the big muscles that once worked her wings and might not eat at all, but she may welcome a drop of honey mixed with water. The next best help you can give her is darkness, warmth and privacy to get on with her job in peace.

Darkness matters to ants. When you're not actually watching them, always block the light out. They also like warmth from above, like sun on the ground.

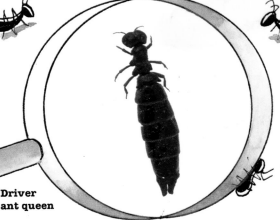

Driver ant queen

When the first workers hatch you'll find out if your set-up is ant-proof! Begin feeding them sugar-water or honey, then try all sorts of crumbs (natural food - ants aren't into E numbers!). Put the food where it's easiest for you - they'll find it, that's what they do best! You can hang a small scrap of raw meat on a paperclip hook. Clear out anything that goes bad.

setting up the ant TERRARIUM

Very soon now, your ants will need some more space. Half-fill your terrarium with soil and sink the nest sandwich in it. Gently ease off one side-sheet (yes, it IS tricky). After a day or two, remove the second side-sheet. Put a few small stones round the edge to encourage the ants to tunnel where you can see them.

Make sure they can't get out and terrorize the family. They'll always come back because the nest is their home, but not a lot of people will believe that!

Once your ants settle down, there will always be something to see. Watch them chat when they meet; try tracking a single ant to see how it spends its day; see if you can work out who goes out hunting, who does the housework, who looks after the nursery...

...and if you feel a really mean mood coming on, you could go out and catch a few wild ants and drop them in for dinner with the home team.

WILD

Panting for ants but never been lucky enough to find a wandering queen? You can still make it. All it takes is a bit of nerve and some plotting and planning.

First, track down some wild ants. Ideally, choose the little black ones. Even more ideally, pick a nest that's a nuisance rather than a colony just minding its own business. Ideally, go for a nest that's easy to get at - there's no need to make things harder than they have to be...

Ant on a stem

READY...

Half-fill your terrarium with loose, dry soil and make sure there's no way out. The first thing wild ants will do is rush around trying **VERY HARD** to escape.

STEADY...

Take a totally ant-proof (which means EVERYTHING-proof) container and a proper digging spade out to your target nest. Then stop and plan your next move carefully. Study the size and shape of the nest for as long as it takes. Remember that it goes down as well as sideways.

GO...

Take a deep breath and dig. Your aim is to cut as big a chunk as possible out of the middle (to make sure of queens) and dump it as unbroken as possible (as fast as possible) into your container. Then seal the container (as fast as possible) and get it home (as fast as possible).

Dump the whole lot into the terrarium and clap the lid on (yes, as fast as possible!). Leave them until they get themselves organised (maybe even a day or two), and then carry on as for the home-grown colony (see p. 14).

Notes for serious ant-watchers

1. There is some stuff called Fluon which ants hate to walk on. Painting this round the top of your formicarium will help to stop them getting out. It's expensive.

2. Ants can't see red light, so if you want to watch your ants all the time instead of just taking the cover off sometimes, use a photographer's red light.

PS. If things with wings start coming up to the surface and milling about, round up some help to shift the whole terrarium outdoors. Then you can take the lid off and let the new queens and drones out to do it all over again.

17

dig THIS

There's a whole lot happening under the ground. Just try dumping a spadeful of soil on to a plastic sheet and see what crawls out.

WRIGGLY THINGIES

Proper worms are pointed at both ends. Earthworms are not hard to miss, but if you have extra-sharp eyes you could also spot some tiny thin white nematode worms. If you find something that's kind of worm-shaped but blunt at the front, it's probably some sort of maggot.

Earthworm

EARTHWORMS

There are different kinds of earthworms. Some little ones are baby big ones, but most small worms are just worms that don't grow big. Check them out (long, short, fat, thin, colour, skin texture?). One sort of worm may turn up in one sort of place (e.g. flowerbeds) and another sort of worm might prefer another sort of place (e.g. under trees).

Have you ever felt a muscular mega-worm walk over your hand? Did you ever put one on a crisp sheet of paper and listen? Then turn one over and have a good look.

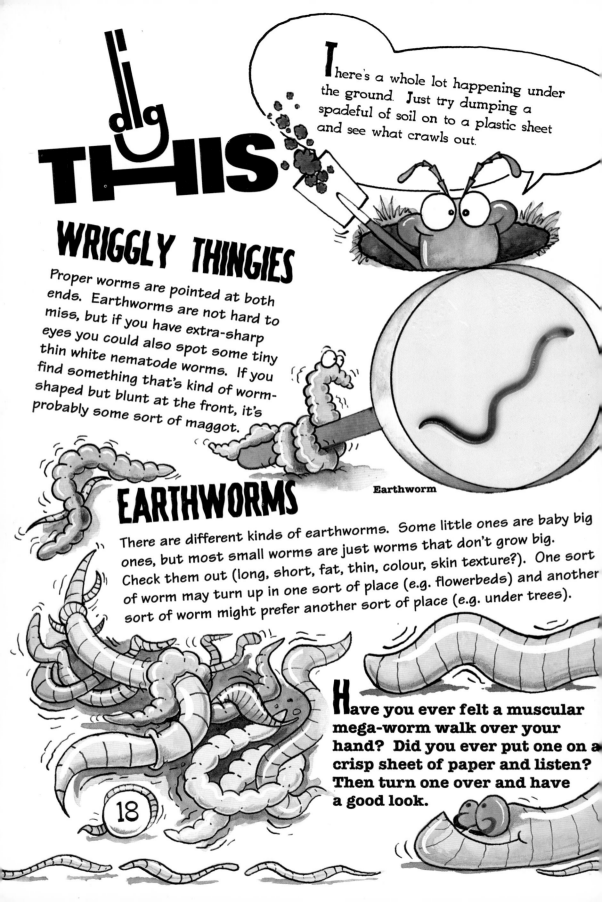

18

You don't see worms sunbathing a lot. They like to be moist and cool and mostly come out on wet nights, which is the best time to find them (oh really?).

On calm, warm, damp nights Mad Jack likes to go out and listen to wild worms hunting. It's wacky but it works. If there's somewhere safe you can go at night, you could try it. Never mind what people think. Nobody will ever guess what you're doing unless you want to tell them (they probably wouldn't believe you anyway!).

Worms are very nervous (no, really); if you hear something that sounds like somebody sucking spaghetti, you can be sure it's a twitchy worm plopping back into its hole (unless somebody IS eating spaghetti out there in the dark, of course...).

When it's dry, worms go down deep. Blackbirds are supposed to tap on the ground to make the worms think it's raining, but nobody knows for sure. When did a blackbird last tell you anything?

RAIN

19

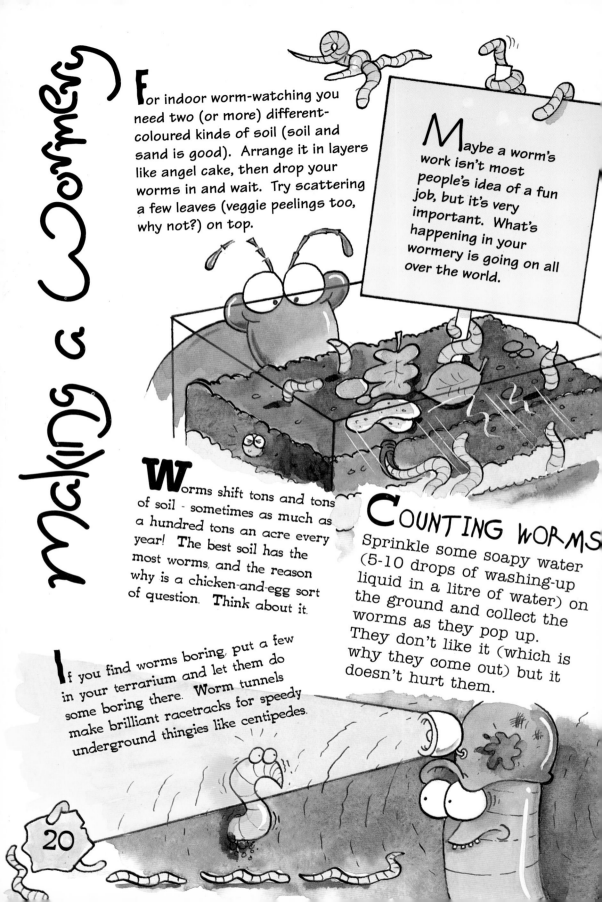

For indoor worm-watching you need two (or more) different-coloured kinds of soil (soil and sand is good). Arrange it in layers like angel cake, then drop your worms in and wait. Try scattering a few leaves (veggie peelings too, why not?) on top.

Maybe a worm's work isn't most people's idea of a fun job, but it's very important. What's happening in your wormery is going on all over the world.

Worms shift tons and tons of soil - sometimes as much as a hundred tons an acre every year! The best soil has the most worms, and the reason why is a chicken-and-egg sort of question. Think about it.

COUNTING WORMS

Sprinkle some soapy water (5-10 drops of washing-up liquid in a litre of water) on the ground and collect the worms as they pop up. They don't like it (which is why they come out) but it doesn't hurt them.

If you find worms boring, put a few in your terrarium and let them do some boring there. Worm tunnels make brilliant racetracks for speedy underground thingies like centipedes.

NEMATODE Worms

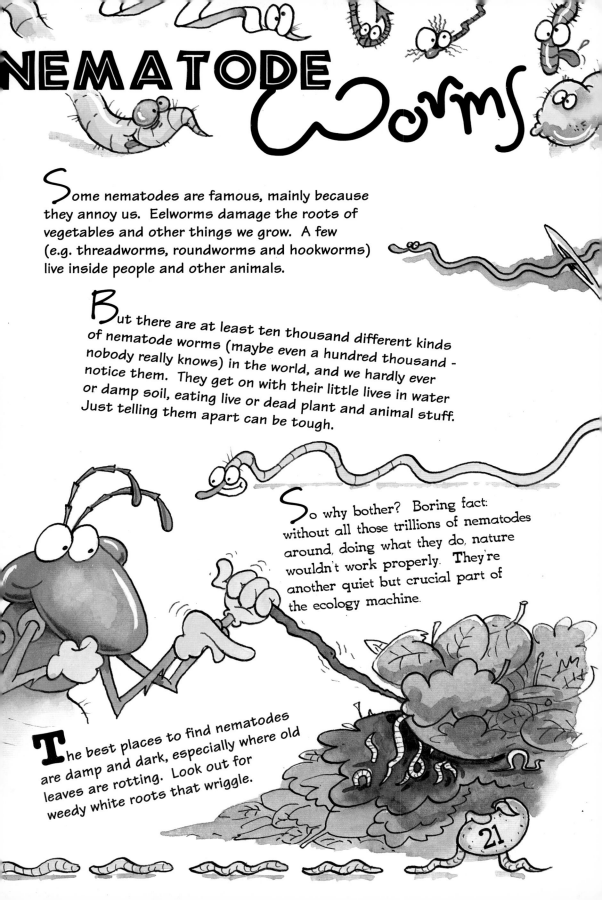

Some nematodes are famous, mainly because they annoy us. Eelworms damage the roots of vegetables and other things we grow. A few (e.g. threadworms, roundworms and hookworms) live inside people and other animals.

But there are at least ten thousand different kinds of nematode worms (maybe even a hundred thousand - nobody really knows) in the world, and we hardly ever notice them. They get on with their little lives in water or damp soil, eating live or dead plant and animal stuff. Just telling them apart can be tough.

So why bother? Boring fact: without all those trillions of nematodes around, doing what they do, nature wouldn't work properly. They're another quiet but crucial part of the ecology machine.

The best places to find nematodes are damp and dark, especially where old leaves are rotting. Look out for weedy white roots that wriggle.

MAGGOTY things

A lot of maggots are the babies (larvae) of insects, and some of them are very hard to tell apart. The best way to find out what they are is to keep them in your terrarium and wait and see what they turn into.

Some maggots (e.g. wireworms and leatherjackets) have names of their own, but most of them don't. Sooner or later, though, every nameless maggot turns into something that does have a name. It'll often become a beetle or a fly.

Maggots

BEEtles

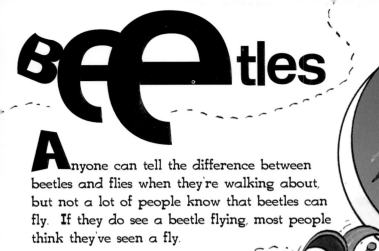

Anyone can tell the difference between beetles and flies when they're walking about, but not a lot of people know that beetles can fly. If they do see a beetle flying, most people think they've seen a fly.

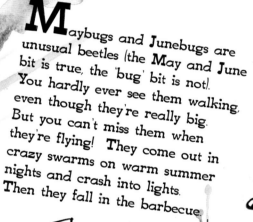

Cockchafer beetle

Most of the time, beetles keep their secret wings folded up under two hard, shiny shells that cover their back.

Maybugs and Junebugs are unusual beetles (the May and June bit is true, the 'bug' bit is not). You hardly ever see them walking, even though they're really big. But you can't miss them when they're flying! They come out in crazy swarms on warm summer nights and crash into lights. Then they fall in the barbecue.

This is a beetle rave. And after two or three years of being maggots, it's not surprising they're ready for some fun - especially when they've suddenly got a pair of humongous wings. So the May and June bugs go for a big night out, dancing with their mates.

23

LADYBIRDS

One of Mad Jack's things is keeping ladybirds. You can even get them to breed in your terrarium. All you need to do is feed them.

Ladybirds eat aphids (greenflies), which also makes them handy to have in the garden. Giving them fresh aphids every day is easier than it sounds because they don't need to be alive. Collect aphids in summer and store them (well-wrapped) in the freezer for later.

Ladybird

Not all ladybirds are red with black spots. Some are black with red spots. Some are totally different - yellow or white, even checked instead of spotted - but it's always easy to see that they're ladybirds by the shape. Try mixing yours up to see if they mate together and make funny-coloured babies.

Making sure you've got males and females is like finding a pair of socks in the dark. The more you collect, the better the chances of getting a pair.

PEAS

24

Ladybird larvae look very different, but they eat aphids just like the adults.

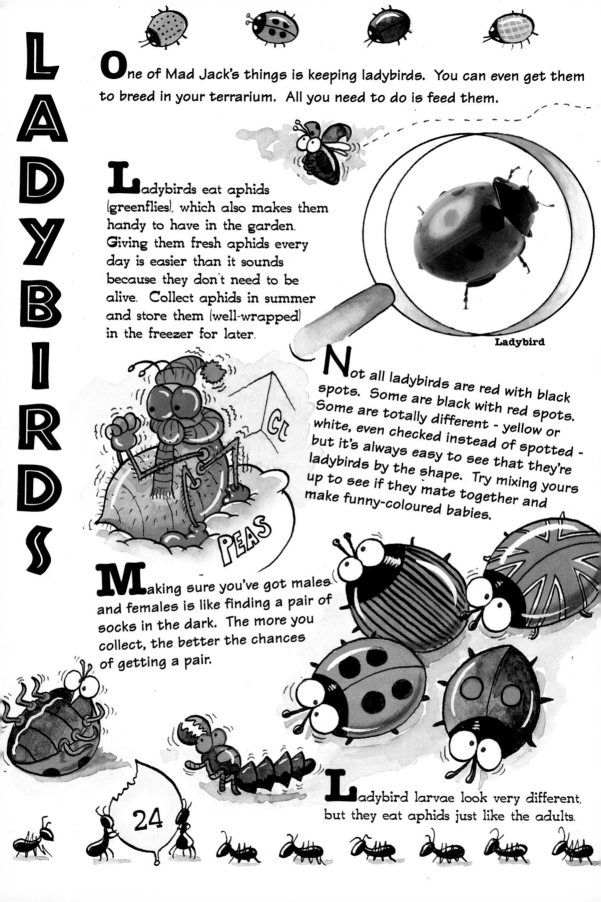

DUNG BEETLE

Dung beetles are a lot more fun than they sound. Some are really big. Most of them are black, but have you ever noticed how many kinds of black there are?

The sacred Egyptian scarab is a big, ball-rolling dung beetle, but you don't have to go to Egypt to get a ball-roller. There are ball-rollers all over the world. If you get one, you can watch it make a perfectly round ball of dung and roll it away to eat in private (well, wouldn't you?). If you get two, you can watch them squabble over their dung-balls.

They'll need feeding (and they eat a lot!) but it's not a problem. Where you find dung beetles, there has to be some of the right sort of dung nearby (think about it). Just remember to look around and collect some dung from the same place as the beetles.

25

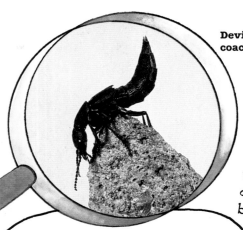

Devil's coach-horse

DEVIL'S COACH-HORSE

Sometimes these long-tailed black beetles come into houses or turn up when you're digging. You need to be quick to catch them, because they really can move! They're terrarium tigers - don't put one in there if you don't want to watch some of the other guests being eaten.

When it's afraid, a devil's coach-horse curls up its tail so it looks like a scorpion. But it's only bluffing; there's no sting in its tail.

The devil's coach-horse is a kind of rove beetle. Rove beetles are built for speed underground, but they still keep a pair of huge wings tucked under those short wing-cases. If they get warm enough, your coach-horses could fly away.

WOOD-BORING beetles

A lot of beetle maggots eat wood. Some come in fantastic colours, and some have extra-long feelers. There are also some very dull little brown ones (woodworms) that can make mincemeat of houses.

Deathwatch beetles (also dull and brown) are a bit bigger than woodworm beetles (and so are their tunnels). The ticking noise they make in summer is the males chatting up females. Females go 'cha-cha-cha-cha' in the spring (not a lot of people know that, because it's very quiet).

Weevils

Weevils are beetles that have a long snout, with a pair of elbowed feelers sticking out halfway down. Their jaws are at the very tip, like a little drill on the end of their nose.

Weevils drill holes to lay their eggs in, so when the maggots hatch out they're safely tucked up inside enough food to last them until they grow up. Then they use their own new jaws to drill their way out.

You could find a weevil maggot quietly stuffing itself inside any part of a plant. Check out anything with a neat round hole in it. Weevil maggots are often tightly curled up, or even folded in half.

Lots of weevils drill into things we eat (e.g. grains, nuts and beans), so you could easily come across some in the larder. Lucky old weevils, having us people to grow so much food for them! Some other lucky old weevils are the boll-weevils that live on cotton plants - there probably wouldn't be a whole lot of cotton in the world if people weren't growing great fields of it to turn into T-shirts and jeans.

27

BUGS

Bugs (YESS - real bugs at last!) look kind of beetle-shaped at first sight, but when you look again you can see quite a lot of differences.

Beetle wing-cases are hard and shiny; bugs' are softer and more leathery-looking. Beetle wing-cases meet tidily all the way down; bugs' cross over at the ends.

Cicada

Bugs' mouths are made for stabbing and sucking instead of biting and chewing. Beetles hardly ever bite but bugs very often stab you - and it hurts!

Bugs come in all shapes and sizes. Some of the largest are the cicadas that make so much noise in hot countries, and some of the smallest are greenflies.

Those itchy lumps you get behind your knees after you've been out pooting are usually bug-bites.

Shield bugs normally stab plants and suck the sap, but that doesn't stop them stabbing people. On the other hand, there are bedbugs, whose main aim in life is to stab people and suck their blood. Bedbugs are a lot rarer nowadays than they once were. Hooray!

Those elegant people in their carriages probably had just one thought in their heads when they stopped at ye olde inne...'Bedbugs!'

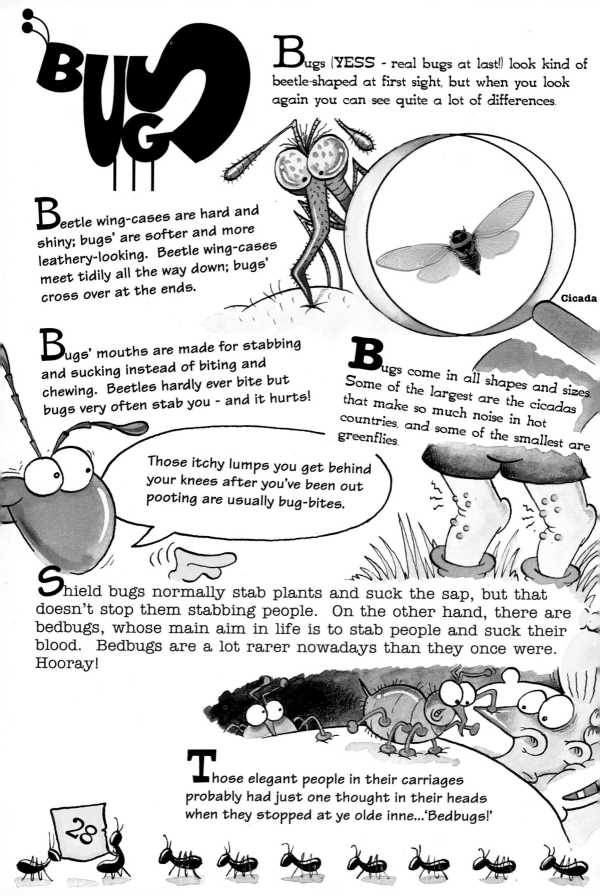

APHIDS

Aphids (greenflies) are small bugs whose mouths are much too weak to pierce human skin. Because they're so soft and juicy, they need all kinds of tricks to stop other thingies eating them. Some (called woolly aphids) cover themselves with waxy fluff, and some make the leaves they're sucking curl up to cover them.

Some of the craftiest aphids bribe ants to protect them. The way they do this is by leaking out some of the sweet sap that they're sucking from a plant. Ants just love sweet stuff, and in return they take good care of the aphids that give it to them! If you happen to notice a lot of ants running up and down a tree, have a look and see you can spot the aphids.

BUGS and BUGS and...more BUGS

Stink bugs, which smell (and taste) awful. Spittle-bugs, which hide under blobs of frothy spit on plant stems. Assassin bugs, which specialise in stabbing all sorts of animals, including people (aaargh!)...

Assassin bug

Leaf-hoppers, Plant-hoppers,

Never heard of them? Well, one sort makes a varnish called shellac, another makes a dye called cochineal, and another (which happens to live in Palestine) makes sweet stuff called 'manna'.

Leaf-hopper

One big difference between bugs and beetles that you can't see right away is that bug babies aren't maggots. They're like little adults without wings. Each time they grow a bit bigger, they have to get out of their old 'suit' and grow a new one to fit.

When is a suit not a suit? When it's a skeleton...

ALAS... I KNEW HIM WELL

The crunchy outside of an insect (or spider, or woodlouse, or other leggy thingy) isn't just a suit of armour. It's the thingie's skeleton - the actual bones its muscles are attached to - as well.

Tree-hoppers... Scale insects

This is a brilliant arrangement, which is why there are such a lot of leggy thingies in the world...

...BUT

Every time a leggy thingy grows a bit bigger, it has to throw away (moult) its whole skeleton and make a new one. And while that's happening it's not only as soft as can be but has no bones at all!

Compared with the way we grow - adding a bit more to our bones day by day - making a whole new skeleton again and again is risky and expensive. Having bones all over is also a lot heavier than having thin ones inside, which is why the biggest leggy thingies live in the sea, where everything weighs less.

These are the main reasons why thingies don't grow as big as elephants or tigers (in case you've ever wondered). To grow that big they'd need to get a skeleton on the inside - and if they did that they'd probably BE elephants or tigers or people, maybe. Um. Enough of that. Time to change the subject.

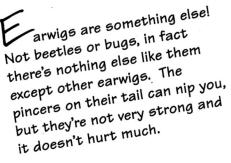

arwigs are something else! Not beetles or bugs, in fact there's nothing else like them except other earwigs. The pincers on their tail can nip you, but they're not very strong and it doesn't hurt much.

Female earwig with eggs

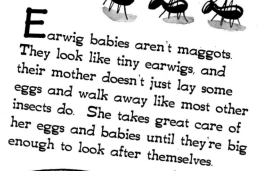

arwig babies aren't maggots. They look like tiny earwigs, and their mother doesn't just lay some eggs and walk away like most other insects do. She takes great care of her eggs and babies until they're big enough to look after themselves.

MAMA!

nother excellent thing about earwigs is that they're not hard to find. Next time you pick something up and an earwig falls out, try not to leap back in horror. This is difficult because it's exactly what the earwig wants you to do so it can get away. Try to catch it instead. Earwigs are a lot more interesting than most people think.

Male &

Male earwigs have very curved pincers and females have straighter ones. If you want earwigs to breed, you'll need both sorts (no, really?).

Female

Feed earwigs on juicy veg like lettuce. If you have a garden, whoever does the gardening will already know what else they like eating! You can set up a simple earwig-trap in the garden with a yoghurt pot on a stick. Just leave it out overnight and collect the 'wigs in the morning.

Finally, be warned that earwigs can fly! They only do it at night so you hardly ever see them doing it - but you quite often find they've gone and done it...or done it and gone...

Silverfish

The tiny shiny thingies that dash away when you switch on the bathroom light are insects, not fish. You knew that, of course. They've also been around about ten times longer than people - and bathrooms as well, obviously.

Other thingies like silverfish (called bristletails) live in dark, damp places all over the place. You could find some in leaf-litter (p. 45).

Silverfish

Silverfish aren't ambitious. They eat whatever's around - wallpaper paste, grot in the bath...anything, really. But if you want to catch a silverfish you need to move like lightning. One good way is to flick it on to a rug, where it gets its feet tangled up, and then poot it up from there. It's a challenge. If you fancy another challenge, try counting its legs.

Once you've got some, you can keep your silverfish in an old chocolate-box; if there are a few crumbs of chocolate left behind in the corners, they won't need feeding for months! There isn't a lot you can do with them after that except look at them sometimes and think deep thoughts about the meaning of life.

THINGIES THAT GO BUMP IN THE NIGHT

A lot of thingies have more sense than to go strolling around in broad daylight getting gobbled up by birds or pooters. But even the night crawlers aren't exactly geniuses. You can catch quite a few of them with this fiendishly simple trap.

Pitfall trap

All you need is a jar with slippery (in)sides and something flat to put over it (to keep out rain and early-birds which could either drown or eat the contents). Bury the jar right up to the rim, prop the lid up on some stones (pick a size that lets in what you want but keeps out bigger thingies that might eat them) and leave it overnight to see what dropped in while you were asleep.

WOODLICE

The oceans are full of crabs, lobsters, shrimps and all sorts of other crustaceans. Why are we suddenly talking about shellfish? Because woodlice, sowbugs and pillbugs are also crustaceans - the only ones that live on dry land - which makes them a bit special.

Rotting wood - especially with bark on - also contains masses of miscellaneous mini-creepies. Poke and poot on the spot or take a chunk home and wait to see what crawls out.

Believe it or not, they have little gills tucked under their shell. Flip one on to its back and count its thrashing legs (if you can!). You should find **7** pairs. You might even have a mother woodlouse with a whole load of eggs stuffed into a pouch near her legs - very like prawns. She keeps them there, in a mini-sea, until the babies are ready for life on land.

Pillbugs are woodlice that curl up and look like shiny - er - well - pills when you disturb them.

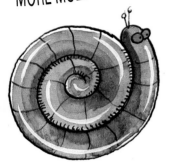

Millipedes

You might find a shiny length of hosepipe with blunt ends, creeping slowly or curled up like a Catherine wheel. Look more closely, and you'll see its body is made up of a string of flexible segments like a shower-hose. Count them if you can.

Millipede

Now multiply by four to get the number of legs your millipede has. There won't be a million - not even a thousand - but there could be a hundred or two. Watch how it organizes all those legs. It doesn't need to hurry because the soft plants it eats can't run away.

Centipedes

A fast, flat, shiny, long-legged thingie is a different animal altogether. If you can count its legs (read the next bit before you try!), you'll probably find around 15 pairs.

Centipedes are desperate hunters with poisonous fangs on their front legs. Centipede venom is strong enough to kill animals bigger than themselves. Drop one in your terrarium and watch it hurtle through worm-tunnels looking for prey. Wait until it catches something. Who needs space monsters?

37

SPIDERS

Eight-legged thingies (clever name Arachnids, aaargh for short) are nearly all meat-eaters. Very few are people-eaters, but most people act as if they all were. If you want to HEAR the difference between 'aaah' and 'aaargh', just show somebody a spider!

House spider

SPIDER PARLOUR

Spiders make brilliant pets. They're easy to keep, easy to feed, and don't have a lot of ambition. The easiest spiders to find, catch (and keep, luckily) are the sort that fall in the bath. Pop one into a big jar (don't forget the airholes) and watch it make its pathetic mess of a web.

The catch

Every now and again your spider will need a fly to eat. The catch is - you have to deliver its dinner alive. Web spiders can't see much. They only really notice things tickling their web, and they'll only go into 'seek and destroy' mode if they feel the special vibes a live fly makes.

& OTHER AAARGHS

Once your spider has made its web it won't be keen to escape. You'll have lots of time to tease a fly into the jar, so you can take it easy. One fly a week is more than enough to keep any spider sleek and fat.

Jaws

Spiders have hollow fangs. They use them (1st) to grab their prey, (2nd) to inject poison and (3rd) to digest fluids, and (last) to suck out the digested insides. These horrible fangs go by the horrible name of chelicerae (pronounced 'kelissary').

eyes

Most spiders have eight bright little eyes, arranged in different patterns. Two are sometimes bigger, and sharp-eyed hunting spiders have a really big pair.

Silk & WEBS

Spider silk is the business. Invisibly thin, impossibly light, incredibly strong - and it only took around 400 million years to get it right! Not all the threads are the same. Some are stretchy and some aren't; some are dotted with sticky-stuff and some aren't. The reason why spiders don't get stuck to their own webs is quite simply because they're careful not to walk on the sticky threads.

Web spiders all do it differently. Each kind has its favourite place and special web style. Look around and see how many different-shaped webs you can find.

Sexing spiders

Male spiders have a blobby pair of feelers; females have a plain pair. (Females are also bigger than males, but this is not a lot of help because old spiders are also bigger than young ones.)

Spider fact:

There are more than 60,000 different spiders in the world. More interesting fact: There are thousands and thousands of spiders everywhere you go. Some clever-clogs worked out that there are 500 billion spiders in Britain! Mad Jack wonders how... Just look around on a misty morning - and remember this is only a giveaway for web spiders.

Not all spiders dangle around in webs. Wolf spiders and jumping spiders go a-hunting. Little zebra spiders quite often prowl around on windowsills indoors; if you're lucky enough to find one, just watch it in action!

Ooooo

Bigger hunting spiders turn up outdoors. You can sometimes find a hunting spider clutching a fuzzy yellow cocoon filled with eggs or speckled with babies. Even bigger ones arrive with the bananas, of course. And in tropical forests there are spiders big enough to eat frogs, mice and birds.

Black widow spider

Some spiders can poison people, but the really big ones are more likely to scare you to death than bite you to death. The most poisonous spiders, like the dreaded black widow, are really quite small.

41

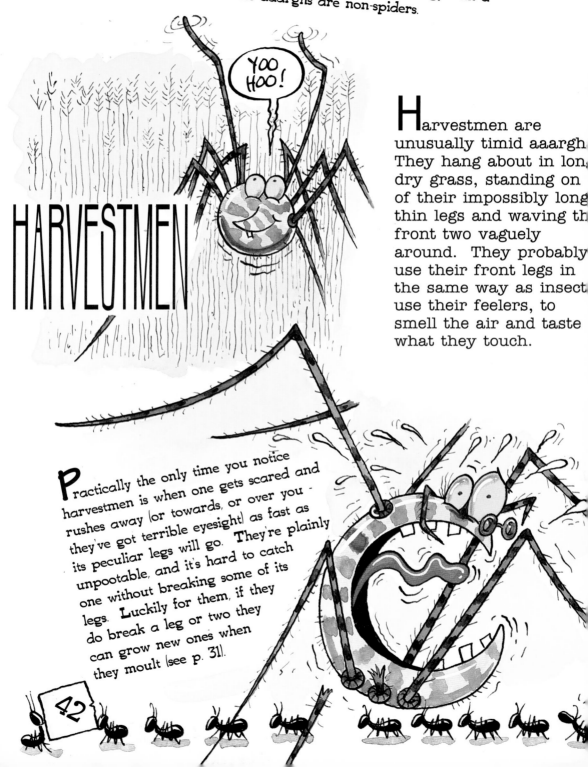

Not everything with 8 legs is a spider. Harvestmen look a bit like spiders but when you look again you can see that their body is just a blob with no waist. Almost every 8-legged thingy with a waist is a spider, all waistless aaarghs are non-spiders.

YOO HOO!

HARVESTMEN

Harvestmen are unusually timid aaargh. They hang about in lon, dry grass, standing on of their impossibly long thin legs and waving th front two vaguely around. They probably use their front legs in the same way as insect use their feelers, to smell the air and taste what they touch.

Practically the only time you notice harvestmen is when one gets scared and rushes away (or towards, or over you - they've got terrible eyesight) as fast as its peculiar legs will go. They're plainly unpootable, and it's hard to catch one without breaking some of its legs. Luckily for them, if they do break a leg or two they can grow new ones when they moult (see p. 31).

(see p. 31)

Besides the waist, the main difference between spiders and mites is a bit like the difference between beetles and bugs. Spiders bite with two jaws; mites and ticks stab with one beak. But they all eat soup.

WAITER!

MITES

TICKS

Spiders liquidise their victims' insides into soup; mites and ticks mostly go for instant soup like sap and blood. Mites are usually a lot smaller than ticks. So now you know. Or do you? Read on.

The easiest mites to spot are the ones called spider mites, red spiders, or money spiders. They're unusual because they feed on plants. Nearly all 8-leggies are meat-eaters, and so are most mites.

We hate the mites called chiggers, because they bite us. Some very tiny mites cause a disease called mange or 'seven-year itch'. But most mites just run around hunting other little thingies. The place where you're most likely to find them is leaf litter (p. 45).

Ticks are bigger. Apart from this, there is another difference we haven't mentioned yet. Before you go pooting, be sure to read page 48.

43

STINGING AAARGHS

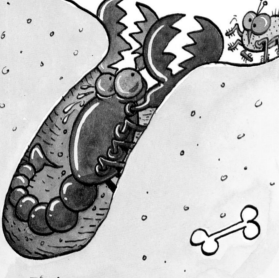

Tail-stingers

Watch out

for scorpions! If one see
you first, this can be bad
news. Little ones are
VERY bad news - they ca
have a nastier sting than
the whoppers, and they
really like to use it. Big
scorpions have big claws
for catching their prey.
They usually save their
stinger for fighting one
another - nobody makes
friends with a scorpion,
not even another
scorpion! The good news
is that scorpions prefer to
live in hot, dry desert-
type places and usually
hide away in burrows
during the day.

Claw-stingers

Scorpions have mini-relatives called
pseudoscorpions (false scorpions). They
don't have a scorpion's stinging tail, but
their claws are loaded with poison instead.
The good news is that these pseuds are
much too small to hurt people - most of
them are so small that they're very hard
to see. But if you do look hard you
could find some just about anywhere
there are other mini-thingies for them to
munch. Look out for them in leaf litter
or old books, under bark and under the
mat - you could even find one hitching a
lift on a fly's leg (how? Read the flypaper!).

LITTLE CRITTERS

The layers of rotting old leaves that pile up under trees, year after year, make happy hunting grounds for pooter-shooters. So do compost heaps.

No trees? No garden?

Try tipping out the grunge in an old flowerpot and go for a pot poot instead.

Springtails

Probably the most abundant (profuse, prolific, plentiful, whatever) animals in the whole world are some mini-thingies hardly anyone has heard of. You can see them any old time, hopping about in leaf litter and old flowerpots, but nearly nobody notices them...

...and they don't even hide. The minute you stir something up, there they are, bouncing around on their little forked tails like bubbles popping on top of a fizzy drink. Just one square foot of ace leaf litter could have five thousand springtails living in it!

Springtails feed on the rotting leaves. Everything else that eats mouldy veg is there, too. And wherever veg-eaters live there are loads of other meat-eating thingies eating them - and each other - all the way up to mega-centipedes and beetles.

So

leaf litter is a great place to look for all sorts of thingies. But sorting out the thingies from the grunge can be tricky. Here's a trick that works especially well for the smallest, shyest thingies.

TULLGREN TUNNEL

Making one of these is a lot easier than saying it. All you need is a funnel (cut the top off a plastic bottle or roll a piece of plastic into a cone shape) and some mesh with holes the right size to hold the grunge but let the thingies out (e.g. the nets that supermarkets put fruit & veg in).
Prop it over a jar, fill with litter, shine a light on top (not so close that everything cooks!) and leave it. If it's working properly most of the thingies will scramble desperately down, away from the light, until they drop into the jar.

Leave some damp paper crumpled in the bottom of the jar for two main reasons: 1. Lotsa litter critters shrivel up and die in the dry; 2. Hiding places help to stop them eating one another before you get a chance to see what you got.

GRUESOME THINGIES

Everythingy has to eat somethingy, and some thingies eat bits of people. Whether a thingy looks gruesome or not depends a lot on where you're coming from.

FLEAS

You'll probably never meet a people-flea, but most people get bitten by a cat-flea sometime. They're amazingly hard to catch and squish. Watch a cat working on its fleas and you'll get the picture.

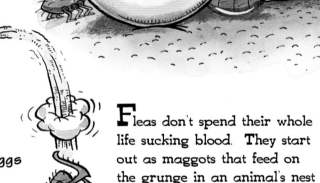

Lice cling, even when they're eggs (nits). They don't all suck blood, but that doesn't make them a lot nicer to meet. Unlike fleas, lice don't bounce about - they can only crawl ever so slowly - so they are hard (or should that be easy?) to 'catch'.

Fleas don't spend their whole life sucking blood. They start out as maggots that feed on the grunge in an animal's nest (or down the side of the sofa).

Hedgehog-fleas are quite soft and easy to squash - maybe because hedgehogs don't go getting their own prickles up their noses chasing fleas!

Some of the most gruesome thingies in the whole world are lice, with their huge claws for gripping on fur or feathers. If you find an old bird's nest in winter, look at it OUTSIDE; don't bring it into the warm!

47

TICKS

Ticks are 8-leggies from hell. They hang around for months, just waiting for the big day when something warm walks by. Most of them go on waiting until they die. You could almost feel sorry for them...

except

...that when a warm body does come along (and it could be you!), that tick is going to grab on with its 8 legs and sink its whole head in you to tank up with blood. A tick can start out as small and white as a rice grain and grow as big as a soaked pea...and it'll turn purple. That's what Mad Jack calls a real yuck!

If you find a tick, DON'T TOUCH IT. If a tick finds you, DON'T TOUCH IT. This is the catch - a tick's beak is barbed like a fish-hook. After waiting so long for a meal that might never arrive, it'll let you break its neck rather than let go. The only way you can make a tick give up is by smothering something it really, really hates on its back.

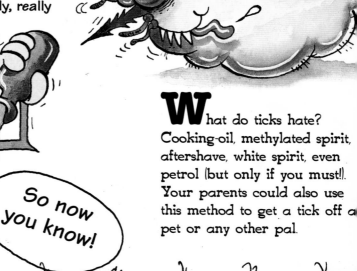

What do ticks hate? Cooking-oil, methylated spirit, aftershave, white spirit, even petrol (but only if you must!). Your parents could also use this method to get a tick off a pet or any other pal.

So now you know!

48